This journal belongs to

Junie B.

and

Lucy

date

1-2018

To my happy, nice friend Shana Corey.
Thank you for helping me with this journal
whenever I got stucked!

XX,

Junie B.

Text and Junie B. doodles copyright © 2003 by Barbara Park.
Illustrations copyright © 2003 by Denise Brunkus.
All rights reserved under International and Pan-American Copyright
Conventions. Published in the United States by Random House Children's
Books, a division of Random House, Inc., New York, and simultaneously
in Canada by Random House of Canada Limited, Toronto.

www.randomhouse.com/kids/junieb

Library of Congress Control Number: 2002106403

ISBN 0-375-82375-1

Printed in the United States of America   First Edition
10 9 8 7 6 5 4 3 2 1

BARBARA PARK

TOP-SECRET
Personal Beeswax

A Journal by <u>Junie B.</u>
(and me!) <u>Lucy T.</u>

with special illustrations by
Denise Brunkus

Random House 🏠 New York

Welcome to Your Journal!

Thank you, journal! Thank you!

I cannot even believe this book!

Mother bought it for me at the store last week! And she said it is not just a book for READING. 'Cause I am allowed to WRITE in it, too!

I always thought writing in books was against the law! On account of one time I drew a wiener sausage in my library book. And the library lady saw it. And I got a note sent home to Mother.

Only take a look at this!

I just drew 2 wiener sausages right on this page! And I'm not even in trouble! ha!

Plus that is not ALL!

'Cause Mother said this book is made for 2 friends to SHARE! And so after I am done with my pages, I am supposed to give it to a friend!

Only here is the problem. I have LOTS of friends. And that includes Y-O-U! (correct?)

And so YOU are my pick!

(Here are the 'structions for you.)

1. First, you are allowed to read the top-secret personal beeswax pages that I wrote. (But you are the ONLY one, and I mean it!)

2. After that, you can fill out your own top-secret personal beeswax pages.

3. Then—when you are all done—you can sign your name on the cover right next to mine! And then this book will be written by only YOU! And only ME! And nobody else! YAY, US!

From your friend,
Junie B. Jones

All About Me: Junie B. Jones !

My name is: Junie B. Jones.
The B stands for Beatrice.
Except I don't like Beatrice.
I just like B and that's all.
My nickname is: Junie B. (Only
when I'm in trouble, my mother calls me
Missy. I don't actually know why.)

If I could have a different name, it would be:
Pedro

My birthday is: Junie the first.

My age is: I am still in my 6's. But pretty
soon, I will be in my 7's, possibly.

My hair is: kind of brownish with reddish
in it. When I sweat, it looks like strings.

My eyes are: the kind of eyes that need
glasses. Both of them are greenish-
bluish. I wish one was brownish. That
would be attractive, I think. 👀

All About Me: _Lucy T._ !

PASTE A PICTURE OF YOURSELF HERE.	**My name is:** _____

My nickname is: _____

_____

If I could have a different name, it would be: _____

My birthday is: _____

My age is: _____

My hair is: _____

My eyes are: _____

Use this page to draw a picture of yourself!

I am good at hair.

Grandma Miller says I am an excellent
drawer. And that is not even bragging
about myself, kind of. ‿

Use this page to draw a picture of yourself!

JUNIE B. 's Family Facts!

(WRITE YOUR NAME HERE.)

My mother's name is: Susan, Susie, Suz, Mommy, and Mother. Plus sometimes Daddy calls her Buttercup. That is ridiculous, I think.

Three words that describe her are:

1. tallish 2. smiley 3. short-hairish

My father's name is: Robert and Bob. His middle name is Dan or Sid or something.

Three words that describe him are:

He loves football.

Other people in my family are: my grampa Frank Miller and his lovely wife, Helen. Also, I have a baby brother named Ollie, and a dog named Tickle.

The thing I like best about my family is:

they seem to enjoy me.

One thing I don't like is: I am not the boss of them.

Except, ha! I AM the boss of Ollie.

_____ 's Family Facts!

PASTE A
FAMILY
PHOTO
HERE.

My mother's name is: _____

_____

_____

_____

Three words that describe her are: _____

_____

PASTE A
FAMILY
PHOTO
HERE.

My father's name is: _____

_____

_____

Three words that describe him are: _____

_____

Other people in my family are: _____

_____

_____

_____

The thing I like best about my family is:

_____

One thing I don't like is: _____

_____

PASTE A
FAMILY
PHOTO
HERE.

Gralnpa Trank Miller

Grandma Helen Miller

Mother

Daddy

This is a picture of baby Ollie. Only
he doesn't actually have devil horns.

Use this frame to draw pictures of your family!

Use this frame to draw pictures of your family!

If I Were the Boss at My House . . .

1. I would make Mother and Daddy go to bed right after dinner.

And . . .

2. I would eat Jell-O with my fingers.

And . . .

3. I would give Ollie to Grampa Miller for keeps, maybe.

And . . .

4. I would go to a bank machine and get free money.

And . . .

5. I would buy a goat, possibly.

3 Rules I Would Change:

First: I would only take a bath when I feel like it. 'Cause every single night, Mother makes me get in the dumb bunny tub. Even when you can't see any dirt on me. And so where is the sense in that, I ask you?

Second: Sometimes I would be allowed to tell a teensy fib. On account of now I am never, ever allowed to tell a fib. Not even when it is absolutely necessary.

Third: I would never go to my room for a time-out. 'Cause time-out is the same thing as jail. And jail is when there is no TV or video games. Plus also, no cell phone, I believe.

If I Were the Boss at My House . . .

1. _____
_____
_____

And . . .

2. _____
_____
_____

And . . .

3. _____
_____
_____

And . . .

4. _____
_____
_____

And . . .

5. _____

3 Rules I Would Change:

First: _____

_____

_____

_____

_____

_____

_____

Second: _____

_____

_____

_____

_____

Third: _____

_____

_____

_____

_____

JUNIE B. 's Fun Friends!
(WRITE YOUR NAME HERE.)

My best friends at school are: Herb, Lennie, José, and not May.

Last year my best friends were: Lucille and that Grace. I still like both of them a real, real lot ... except not Lucille.

I like my friends because: all of us have the same sense of humorous, mostly.

Lennie

Herb

José

Use these frames to draw or paste pictures of your friends!

Here are some other people I like: Shirley and Roger and Sheldon, and still not May.

The thing I like to do best with my friends is: just plain old regular stuff, like talking and laughing and playing on the playground. But even when we don't do anything at all, we still have fun together.

That Grace

Richie Lucille

Not May

_____'s Fun Friends!

(WRITE YOUR NAME HERE.)

My best friends at school are: _____

_____

Last year my best friends were: _____

_____

_____

I like my friends because: _____

_____

_____

Use these frames to draw or
paste pictures of your friends!

Here are some other people I like: _____

_____

The thing I like to do best with my friends is: _____

_____

_____

_____

_____

_____

Friends on a Picnic!

Here is a story about a picnic! Fill in the blanks
to make the story about you and your friends!

Once upon a time, there were _four_ special friends.
Their names were _Herb and Lennie and José_
and Junie B., and not May .

One day, they decided to have a picnic at the
park.

"Oh, boy! A picnic!" said _José_ . "Let's
bring all our favorite foods!"

"Okay!" said _Junie B._ . "I will bring _a_
delicious lemon pie ."

"And I will bring _a cheese sandwich_ ,"
said _Herbert_ .

"Mmm-mmm! And I will bring _pasketti and_
meatballs !" said _Lennie_ .

"I will bring _sugar cookies_ !" said _José_ .

The next day, the friends took their picnic to the
park. They spread their blanket under a shady
elephant with a big trunk.

Pretty soon, the weather started to change. The sun disappeared and black clouds rolled in.

The air grew __hair__.

Then, all of a sudden, there was a loud clap of __clapping__.

The friends looked up.

PLOP! PLOP! PLOP!

Wet drops splashed on their __eyeballs__.

"Oh no! It's starting to __plop__!" said __Herbert__. "Our picnic will be ruined!"

It was __Junie B. Jones__ to the rescue!

"No, it won't! I will save the day!" __she__ said.

Then, quick as a flash, __Junie B.__ reached into the picnic basket and pulled out a handy little __giant piece of cardboard__.

"I carry this with me everywhere I go, so I NEVER get rained on!" __Junie B.__ declared.

__She__ hurried and raised it over their heads.

Then all of the friends stayed cozy and dry until the rain finally stopped.

It was the __funnest__ picnic ever!

The End

Friends on a Picnic!

Here is a story about a picnic! Fill in the blanks to make the story about you and your friends!

Once upon a time, there were _5_ special friends. Their names were _Sam, Scarlett, Stella, Mariam and Lucy_.

One day, they decided to have a picnic at the park.

"Oh, boy! A picnic!" said _Sam_. "Let's bring all our favorite foods!"

"Okay!" said _Lucy_. "I will bring _pumkin pie_."

"And I will bring _snadichwis_," said _Scarlett_.

"Mmm-mmm! And I will bring _green grapes_!" said _Mariam_.

"I will bring _Juice boxs_!" said _Stella_.

The next day, the friends took their picnic to the park. They spread their blanket under a shady _tree_ with a big trunk.

Pretty soon, the weather started to change.

The sun disappeared and black clouds rolled in.

The air grew ___cold___ .

Then, all of a sudden, there was a loud clap of

___thunder___ .

The friends looked up.

PLOP! PLOP! PLOP!

Wet drops splashed on their ___knees___ .

"Uh no! It's starting to ___rain___ !" said

___Sam___ . "Our picnic will be ruined!"

It was ___Lucy___ to the rescue!

"No, it won't! I will save the day!" ___Lucy___ said.

Then, quick as a flash, ___Lucy___ reached

into the picnic basket and pulled out a handy little

___umbrella___ .

"I carry this with me everywhere I go, so I NEVER

get rained on!" ___Lucy___ declared.

___She___ hurried and raised it over their heads.

Then all of the friends stayed cozy and dry until

the rain finally stopped.

It was the ___best___ picnic ever!

___The End___

School Days!

I am in Ist **grade.** (First means you are the winner!)

The name of my school is: Clarence somebody or other Elementary School.

This is how I get to school: I ride the bus, of course. I ride it every single day. Except for I don't actually ride on Saturday or Sunday or on weekends.

My favorite thing about school is: when my teacher draws a happy face (☺) on my paper. Also, I enjoy drinking from the water fountain.

My least favorite thing about school is: Tattletale May

I sit next to: Yeah, only too bad for me, because the answer is Tattletale May again.

My teacher's name is: Mr. Scary. He made that name up, I believe.

~~Three~~ 5 **words that describe my teacher are:** He is a man teacher.

The thing I like best about my teacher is: His voice is very calmy. Also, I like his mustache.

This is what my teacher looks like:

This is a close-up of just his mustache! ha!

(DRAW OR PASTE A PICTURE OF YOUR TEACHER HERE.)

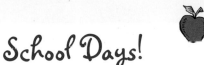

School Days!

 I am in _____ grade. _____

_____

 The name of my school is: _____

_____

 This is how I get to school: _____

_____

 _____

_____

 My favorite thing about school is: _____

_____

 _____

_____

 My least favorite thing about school is: _____

_____

_____

 _____

 I sit next to: _____

_____

_____

My teacher's name is: _____

Three words that describe my teacher are: _____

The thing I like best about my teacher is: _____

This is what my teacher looks like:

(DRAW OR PASTE A PICTURE OF YOUR TEACHER HERE.)

If I Ruled the School . . .

My new name would be _Queen I Am the Boss of You._

Whenever I walked down the hall, everyone would have to bow and _give me sugar cookies._

I would wear a crown made out of _shiny yold glitter._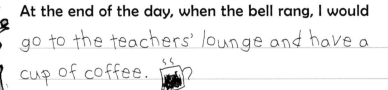

My long royal robe would be made out of _my skirt that looks like velvet._

There would be a golden throne in the _school cafeteria._

I would sit there each day and _eat pie and rule._

Each day for lunch, I would have _a meatball._

At the end of the day, when the bell rang, I would _go to the teachers' lounge and have a cup of coffee._

4 New School Rules I Would Make Are:

1. No walking in the hall. You are only allowed to run, and that's all. Plus occasionally, there will be fast skipping.

2. Sleep late in the morning and watch cartoons. Then come to school whenever you feel like it. We will still be open, probably.

3. If you actually don't feel like doing your work, please get up and wander around the room. Thank you.

4. There are free doughnuts in the cafeteria. Please drop by and pick one up. On Fridays— FREE ORANGE SODA!

If I Ruled the School . . .

My new name would be _____

_____

Whenever I walked down the hall, everyone would

have to bow and _____

_____

I would wear a crown made out of _____

_____

My long royal robe would be made out of _____

_____

There would be a golden throne in the _____

_____

I would sit there each day and _____

_____

Each day for lunch, I would have _____

_____

At the end of the day, when the bell rang, I would

_____

_____

4 New School Rules
I Would Make Are:

1. _____

_____

_____

_____

2. _____

_____

_____

_____

3. _____

_____

_____

_____

4. _____

_____

_____

_____

_____

Pets on Parade!

My favorite pet is. my dog named Tickle.

We've had that guy **since** before I got borned.

My pet's color is: fuzzy furry yellow.

My favorite thing to do with my pet is: I love it when Mother lets me take him for a walk. She lets me hold the leash all by myself. It is very fun, usually. Only I don't actually like it when Tickle sees a cat. 'Cause then he pulls me off my feet. And both of us go zooming through people's yards. Plus sometimes I fall down. And so what do you know? Maybe walking Tickle all by myself is not actually my favorite thing after all. So just forget this whole entire answer.

Sometimes I catch my pet staring at me. When this

happens, I bet _Tickle_ **is thinking:**

(WRITE YOUR PET'S NAME.)

You are my favorite
person in this whole entire
family, Junie B. Jones. I am a
lucky duck to have you. I think this
family was funner before baby Ollie came
to live here. He smells like stink. Did you
ever notice that? Sometimes I wish that
I had another puppy to play with. Hey!
Maybe you can beg Mother and Daddy
to get one! Then we can name him Vic!
And Vic will be all yours. And all
mine. And NOT Ollie's. ha!
The end. Bow wow.

(DRAW OR PASTE A PICTURE OF YOUR PET HERE.)

Pets on Parade!

My favorite pet is. _____

_____

We've had _____ since

_____

My pet's color is: _____

_____

My favorite thing to do with my pet is: _____

_____

_____

_____

_____

_____

_____

_____

_____

_____

_____

_____

Sometimes I catch my pet staring at me. When this happens, I bet _____ is thinking:

(WRITE YOUR PET'S NAME.)

_____

_____

_____

_____

_____

_____

_____

_____

_____

_____

_____

(DRAW OR PASTE A PICTURE OF YOUR PET HERE.)

My House!

When I look out the window of my house, I see:
what is outside, that's what. Like I am
looking out there right now. And some
of the stuff I see is:
(1) First I see a tree.
(2) Two, I see some garbage cans.
(3) Three, I see the lady across the
street. She is hollering at her
husband. 'Cause he doesn't want to
mow the grass, apparently. But that is
NOT her job, mister!

**If I could change one thing about my house, it
would be:** I would make it into a
beautiful castle with water all around
the outside. There would be a popcorn
machine in the living room. Plus also,
I would have a candy counter and
sell nachos.

Draw a picture of where you live!

My House!

When I look out the window of my house, I see:

_____

_____

_____

_____

_____

_____

_____

_____

_____

If I could change one thing about my house, it

would be: _____

_____

_____

_____

_____

Draw a picture of where you live!

My Room!

The color of my room is: My walls are bluish greenish. Mother picked out that color on account of she said it matches my eyes. That was a nice gesture by her, I think. My furniture color is bluish-greenish, too-ish. I wish it was whitish.

I share my room with: all of my stuffed animals. Also, sometimes I let my dog named Tickle take naps on my bed. Only he's not actually allowed up there. But he really, really loves it. And so me and him keep his naps a secret from Mother.

My closet: smells like feet.

I love my room because: yeah, only here's the trouble. I don't actually love it that much. 'Cause I want a canopy

I didn't have a room picture. So here is Philip Johnny Bob instead. He lives there!

bed very bad. But Mother keeps saying no, no, no. And so all I have is just a plain old regular bed. And a plain old regular desk. And a plain old regular dresser. And that is just a plain old regular room.

(DRAW OR PASTE A PICTURE OF YOUR ROOM HERE.)

My favorite thing to do in my room is: I like to talk to my stuffed elephant named Philip Johnny Bob. Also, I like to talk to my teddy, and my Raggedy Ann named Ruth, and my Raggedy Andy named Larry. But Philip Johnny Bob is the smartest out of all of those guys. You can tell by what he says.

My Room!

The color of my room is:

_____

_____

_____

_____

_____

_____

I share my room with:

_____

_____

_____

_____

_____

_____

My closet:

_____

I love my room because:

_____

_____

_____

_____

_____

_____

_____

_____

_____

_____

(DRAW OR PASTE A PICTURE
OF YOUR ROOM HERE.)

My favorite thing to do in my room is: _____

_____

_____

_____

_____

_____

_____

Favorites and "Unfavorites"!

My favorite color is: Mostly it's the color purple. But sometimes it is the color red. And so those two colors will just have to share me, I guess.
P.S. Also, I am fond of sky blue pink.

My "unfavorite" color is: the color of bruise. 'Cause yesterday I bumped my leg on the bus step. And today my skin is black and blue. And so at school, Lucille pointed at it, and she said ICK!
   That's how come I wish my bruise could be sky blue pink. Then all the children would look at it and say OOOOOH, PRETTY!

My favorite animal is: My favorite animal used to be a baby pet monkey. But then I saw a show on baby pet monkeys. And bad news. They grow up to be big pet monkeys. Plus also, they get teeth. And so now my favorite animal is any kind that doesn't grow up and just has gums.

My "unfavorite" animal is: birds that peck your head into a nub. Also, I don't like the kind of tuna fish that is canned in oil.

My favorite game is: The funnest game I love is playing tag with my baby brother named Ollie. 'Cause he can't even run yet. And so all I have to do is tag him and he stays "it" forever. Then I go watch TV.

My "unfavorite" game is: I do not like dodgeball. 'Cause who likes getting hit in the head by a ball? That's what I would like to know.

Favorites and "Unfavorites"!

My favorite color is: _____

_____

_____

_____

_____

_____

My "unfavorite" color is: _____

_____

_____

_____

_____

_____

_____

_____

_____

My favorite animal is: _____

_____

_____

_____

My "unfavorite" animal is: _____

My favorite game is: _____

My "unfavorite" game is: _____

Food I Love!

This is my mouth watering! ha! ↓

The food I love best is <u>yummy, delicious lemon pie!</u> When I grow up, I am going to eat <u>lemon pie</u> for breakfast, lunch, and dinner! Here is a poem about my favorite food! It is called:

I LOVE
YUMMY, DELICIOUS LEMON PIE

by <u>Junie B. Jones</u>

Roses are <u>red.</u>
Violets are <u>blue.</u>
I love <u>yummy, delicious lemon pie.</u>
And so <u>does my grampa Frank Miller.</u>

(P.S. Yeah, only my poem didn't actually rhyme that good. 'Cause pie and Miller don't sound like each other. But I cannot control that situation.)

More Food I Love!

1. First, I love pasketti and meatballs! I love to sprinkle cheese on the top of it. I pile it up until Daddy yells, "WHOA! WHOA! WHOA, MISSY!" That means STOP the cheese, apparently.

Here is a variety of meatballs.

2. Next, I love the kind of whipped cream that comes in a can. Sometimes I squirt it into my mouth till my cheeks fill up. I mostly just do this when Mother is in the shower.

3. The number three thing I love is a Swish cheese sandwich. Swish cheese is very holey. I do not know the cause of this trouble. Sometimes I stick my tongue through the holes and wiggle it at Mother. That is called comedy.

Food I Love!

The food I love best is _____

_____ When I grow up, I am going

to eat _____ for breakfast,

lunch, and dinner! Here is a poem about my

favorite food! It is called:

I LOVE

_____

by _____

Roses are _____

Violets are _____

I love _____

And so _____

More Food I Love!

1.

2.

3.

Recipe Fun!

Here is a special recipe card just for you.
Write a recipe of something delicious
that you know how to make!

SWISH CHEESE SANDWICH

1. get 2 breads
2. get 3 Swish cheeses
3. get mustard and mayonnaise
4. put mustard and mayonnaise on the breads
5. put the breads around the Swish cheeses
6. Okay, that is the end of what you do.
   THE END

Draw a picture of your recipe here!

Chips and pickles

Swish Cheese Sandwich

(TITLE OF YOUR PICTURE)

Recipe Fun!

Here is a special recipe card just for you.
Write a recipe of something delicious
that you know how to make!

Draw a picture of your recipe here!

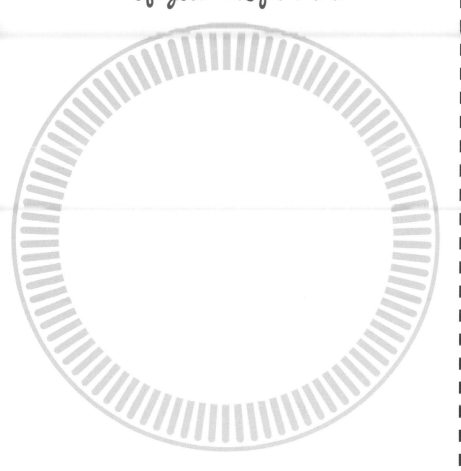

_____

(TITLE OF YOUR PICTURE)

Things That Make Me NERVOUS!

1. The first thing that makes me nervous is ponies.

Here's why: 'Cause ponies can stomple you into the ground and kill you, that's why. Only Mother says that has never actually happened before, probably. But she is not even a pony expert.

2. The next thing that makes me nervous is roosters.

Here's why: 'Cause roosters have sharp lips, and a terrible attitude.

3. The number three thing is CLOWNS! CLOWNS! CLOWNS!

Here's why: On account of clown lips are

very too red. And their teeth are very too yellow. Plus also, I do not enjoy their giant feet.

4. Next, I am nervous about monsters under my bed.

Here's why: 'Cause if you hang your piggy toes over the side of your bed, the monsters will think they are little wiener sausages. And they will eat them. Also, monsters drool on your pillowcase while you are sleeping. I have felt this for a fact.

5. The last thing I am nervous of is getting chocolate milk poured on my head when I'm riding home on the bus.

Here's why: I don't think this one actually needs explaining.

Things That
Make Me
NERVOUS!

THIS IS ME
WHEN I'M NERVOUS.

1. _____

_____

_____

Here's why: _____

_____

_____

_____

_____

_____

_____

2. _____

_____

Here's why: _____

_____

3. _____

_____

Here's why: _____

4. _____

_____

Here's why: _____

_____

_____

_____

_____

_____

_____

5. _____

_____

_____

Here's why: _____

_____

Free Drawing Pages!

Use these pages to show off your artistic talent!

Queen I Am the Boss of You

Other stuff that I draw really good

Free Drawing Pages!

Use these pages to show off your artistic talent!

Switcheroo!

Did you ever wish you had a different name?

What if you could change your name?

Better yet . . . what if you could change EVERYONE'S name?

Person	Current Name	Brand-new Name!
Mother	Susan	Xena, Warrior Princess
Father	Robert	Lance
Brother	Ollie	Stinky
Sister		Junie Junior
Grandmother	Helen	Pinkie
Grandfather	Frank	Skippy
Best Friend	Herbert	Herbert is already perfect.
Teacher	Mr. Scary	Mr. Mustache
Others:		
Cafeteria Lady	Mrs. Gladys Gutzman	(I LOVE that name just like it is.)

And Don't Forget These!

"Non-Person"	Current Name	Brand-new Name!
Dog	Tickle	Ralph Johnson
Cat		Sneaky Pete
Fish	Fish Stick	Mr. Paul
Bird	Twitter	Birdbrain
Teddy Bear	Teddy	Glu
Others:		
Elephant	Philip Johnny Bob	Mufasa
Raggedy Andy	Larry	Homer
Raggedy Ann	Ruth	Marye

Switcheroo!

Did you ever wish you had a different name?

What if you could change your name?

Better yet . . . what if you could change

EVERYONE'S name?

Person	Current Name	Brand-new Name!
Mother		
Father		
Brother		
Sister		
Grandmother		
Grandfather		
Best Friend		
Teacher		
Others:		

And Don't Forget These!

"Non-Person"	Current Name	Brand-new Name!
Dog		
Cat		
Fish		
Bird		
Teddy bear		
Others:		

I Smile When I Remember the Time That . . .

Me and my grampa Frank Miller ate a whole entire lemon pie for dinner. Just PIE, I mean. And NOTHING else! It happened the night my baby brother named Ollie got borned. 'Cause my grandma was at the hospital with Mother and Daddy. And so hurray, hurray! Me and my grampa Miller got to stay all by ourselves without a babysitter! And so Grampa smoked a stinky cigar right in the house! And he didn't even get yelled at! And then he let me put on my grandma's red high heels and her hat with the long brown feather!

Only pretty soon, all of that fun made us hungry. And so I ran to the kitchen and opened up the 'frigerator

door. And wowie wowie wow! There was a
big fat lemon pie in there!

   I called to my grampa. "HEY, FRANK!
THERE'S A BIG FAT LEMON PIE IN
HERE!" I yelled. And so Grampa Miller
hurried right into the kitchen. And he
put the pie on the table. And then me
and him ate the whole thing right out of
the pan!

   And here is the funnest part of all!
WE DIDN'T EVEN GET CAUGHT!
'Cause Grampa Miller told my grandma
that THE CAT ATE IT! Only here is the
joke! They don't even HAVE a cat! So
that is not even a fib, probably! Ha!

   I love that darned story. The memory
of it makes me smile and smile.

      The End   ☺   ☺

I Smile When I Remember the Time That . . .

Grown-ups Are
WEIRD Because:

1. Because grown-ups say stuff that doesn't even make sense, that's why. Like one time, my grandma Helen Miller asked me if the cat got my tongue. And that made me feel sick inside. 'Cause what kind of a cat wants to eat people's tongues, I ask you? Disgusto Cat, that's who.

2. Plus another thing that's weird about grown-ups is when Mother says I can't have dessert unless I finish my dinner. 'Cause dessert is an important PART of dinner. And so how can I finish my dinner if I'm not allowed to eat my dessert? Huh? Did anyone ever think of that problem?

Grown-ups Are
FUN Because:

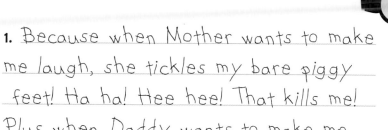

1. Because when Mother wants to make me laugh, she tickles my bare piggy feet! Ha ha! Hee hee! That kills me! Plus when Daddy wants to make me laugh, he makes loud pig snorts and he chases me around the room. Our family gets a kick out of pig humor, apparently.

Oink!

2. Another time grown-ups are fun is when daddies ride you on their shoulders. 'Cause you feel big as the trees up there! Only I don't actually like it when I crash into stuff. Also, sometimes when I get tired of walking in the mall, Daddy gives me a piggyback ride. And so guess what? More piggy humor!

Grown-ups Are **WEIRD** Because:

1. _____

_____

_____

_____

_____

_____

_____

_____

_____

2. _____

_____

_____

_____

_____

_____

_____

_____

_____

_____

_____

Grown-ups Are
FUN Because:

1. _____

_____

_____

_____

_____

_____

_____

2. _____

_____

_____

_____

_____

_____

_____

Haiku to You!

Haiku is a Japanese form of poetry.
The poems are often about nature or something
peaceful. Usually they have three lines.

1. Line one has 5 syllables.

2. Line two has 7 syllables.

3. Line three is back to 5 syllables.

Here is one example:

WINTER

Silent snowflakes fall
On freezing, icy fingers.
Holes in my mittens.

Now write your own haiku!

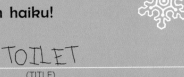

TOILET
(TITLE)

by _____ Junie B. Jones

Noisy water runs
out in a swishy, fast flush.
Hole in the bottom.

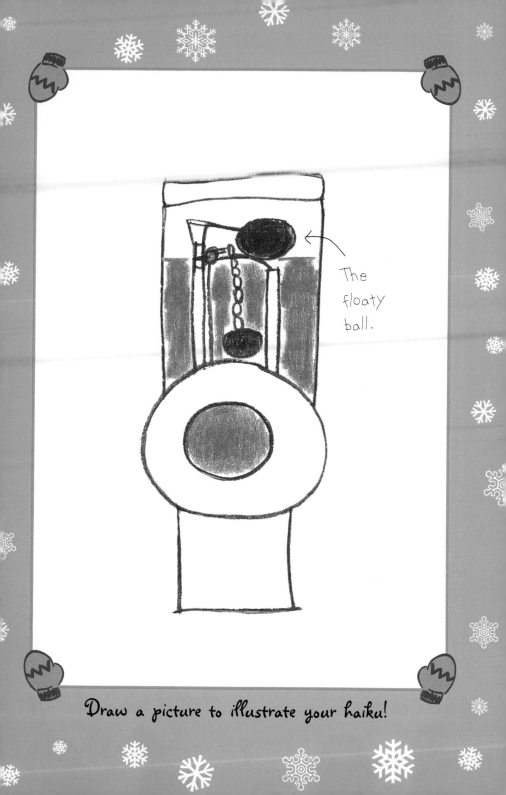

The
floaty
ball.

Draw a picture to illustrate your haiku!

Haiku to You!

Haiku is a Japanese form of poetry. The poems are often about nature or something peaceful. Usually they have three lines.

1. Line one has 5 syllables.

2. Line two has 7 syllables.

3. Line three is back to 5 syllables.

Here is one example:

WINTER

Silent snowflakes fall
On freezing, icy fingers.
Holes in my mittens.

Now write your own haiku!

_____
(TITLE)

by _____

_____

_____

_____

Draw a picture to illustrate your haiku!

Two Pages All Your Own!
Here are two free pages
to write anything you want!

1. Here is something I thought of this morning when I was coloring at the breakfast table. 'Cause my grampa Miller was eating a bowl of prunes and a danish. And so if I could make a brand-new crayon color, I would make the color of PRUNISH. 'Cause Grampa would really love that color, I bet. I would call it Frank Miller.

2. Here is a little secret I am keeping. Last week I told a teensy fib to Mother. And she didn't even catch me. Only now I am feeling bad inside. And so I should tell her I fibbed, probably. Only I don't actually want to get in trouble. And so I will just tell her here instead. And that

will be almost as good, kind of.

Dear Mother,
I am sorry I told you a fib last week.
'Cause I accidentally told you that
Tickle put Ollie in the hall closet. Only
it was actually me who did that. On
account of that baby kept crying his
head off for no good reason. And so
I just put him in the closet for a
teensy second. But I didn't even shut
the door all the way. Plus Ollie even
likes it in there, I think. 'Cause when
I peeked in at him, he was sitting on
the vacuum cleaner very happy.
                    Love, your girl,
                    Junie B. Jones
P.S. I am glad we had this talk.

Two Pages All Your Own!

Here are two free pages to write anything you want!

 # Knock, knock.

Do you have a favorite knock, knock joke?
Write it down!
Or even better, make up some of your own!

Knock, knock.

Who's there?

Hatch

Hatch who?

Ha ha!

Made you sneeze!

Knock, knock.

Who's there?

Iris

Iris who?

Iris I was an

Oscar Mayer wiener!

Knock, knock.

Who's there?

Snot

Snot who?

Snot polite

to say snot!

Knock, knock.

Who's there?

Isadora

Isadora who?

Isadora locked
or can I come in?

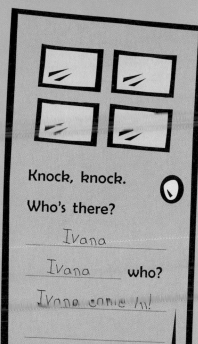

Knock, knock.

Who's there?

Ivana

Ivana who?

Ivana come in!

Knock, knock.

Who's there?

Wet

Wet who?

Wet me in!

It's waining!

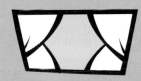

Knock, knock.

Who's there?

Issue

Issue who?

Issue glad
to see me?

 # Knock, knock.

Do you have a favorite knock, knock joke?

Write it down!

Or even better, make up some of your own!

Knock, knock.

Who's there?

_____
_____ who?
_____
_____

Knock, knock.

Who's there?

_____
_____ who?
_____
_____

Knock, knock.

Who's there?

_____
_____ who?
_____
_____

Knock, knock.
Who's there?
_____
_____ who?
_____

Knock, knock.
Who's there?
_____
_____ who?
_____
_____

Knock, knock.
Who's there?
_____
_____ who?
_____
_____

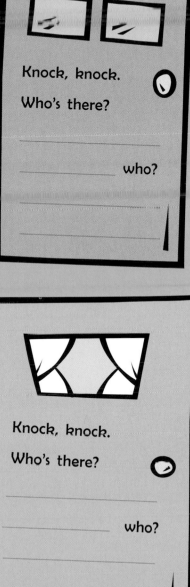

Knock, knock.
Who's there?
_____
_____ who?
_____
_____

MORE Favorites!

My favorite smell is: the smell of dinner cooking. 'Cause sometimes I get hungry as a moose. And I start to whine, "I'M HUNGRY, I'M HUNGRY, I'M HUNGRY!" And then, all of a sudden, I sniff the air. And there's hamburgers cooking in the kitchen! Yum! That smell makes my mouth smile, I tell you! Plus also, it makes me drooly. DROOLY is a nice compliment, I believe.

My favorite insects are: I mostly just like ladybugs and butterflies and that's all. Also, I never step on earthworms. 'Cause Mother says that earthworms are our friends. Plus also, I don't want squished worms stuck to my feet.

My favorite fruit is: Froot Loops. Also, I like cherry Jell-O and grape Kool-Aid

and orange Popsicles and lemon pie
and strawberry shortcake and
raspberry sherbet and blueberry
pancakes and peach cobbler and
banana muffins and chocolate-covered
raisins.
    Fruit is very nutritious.

My favorite ~~farm-animal sound~~ is: part of the toilet   Yeah, only
I don't even live on a farm, so I had
to change this one. And so my
favorite part of the toilet is the
floaty ball. The flouty ball is in the
tank part. It is fun to watch that
 thing. 'Cause when the water gets
flushed, the ball goes down. And then
more water comes in! And ha! Up it
floats again! I would love to meet the
guy who thought of that entertaining
invention.

MORE Favorites!

My favorite smell is: _____

_____

_____

_____

_____

_____

_____

_____

_____

_____

_____

_____

My favorite insects are: _____

_____

_____

_____

_____

My favorite fruit is: _____

_____

My favorite farm animal sound is:

Feeling My Feelings!
EMBARRASSMENT

Embarrassment feels: hottish and reddish and sweatish.

One of my most embarrassing moments ever was when: me and my mother were in the grocery store. And this lady had the 'zact same color coat as Mother. So too bad for me, 'cause I accidentally grabbed the lady's hand by mistake.

Plus also, I lifted up my feet and I dangled from her arm.

That's when the lady hollered, "OW!" And she shook me off of her. Then Mother came running over. And she said a 'pology to the lady.

After that, both of them stared

and stared at me.

My face turned reddish and hottish and sweatish.

I hid my head in my sweater sleeve.

Then finally, the lady smiled a teensy bit. And Mother smiled, too.

Only I didn't smile at all. 'Cause embarrassment is only smiley if it happens to a different kid. And not you.

Plus grown-ups should make their coats different, I think.

The End

Feeling My Feelings!

EMBARRASSMENT

Embarrassment feels: _____

_____

_____

One of my most embarrassing moments ever

was when: _____

_____

_____

_____

_____

_____

_____

_____

_____

_____

_____

_____

_____

_____

_____

_____

_____

_____

THIS IS ME WHEN
I'M EMBARRASSED.

_____

_____

_____

_____

_____

_____

_____

_____

_____

_____

_____

_____

More About Feelings . . .
SAD AND BLUE

Sometimes when I am sad and blue:

I don't remember what happy feels like.

Some things that make me sad, and why:

1. When kids at school call me a mean name. I hate that. 'Cause then I have to call them a mean name back. And then they call me an even meaner name. And so I call them a meaner name, too. And pretty soon, we have called each other every mean name in the book. Only what do you know? Nobody is the winner.

2. A different thing that makes me sad is when Bambi's mother got killed in that deer movie. Also, I didn't like it when the Lion King dad died, either. 'Cause even though cartoons aren't

real, I still love those people.

3. Here is something else I thought of. It really makes me sad when I have to move to a different city and go to a different school. 'Cause then I will never see my bestest friend named Herb again. Only that has never actually happened to me before. But if it does, I am not going to be pleasant about it.

4. The number four thing that makes me sad is when Mother and Daddy argue. I hate that a real lot. But Mother keeps saying that all parents in the whole world argue sometimes. Only what does that got to do with anything? 'Cause Mother and Daddy are not all parents. And so they should just behave theirselves and act nice.

More About Feelings . . .

SAD AND BLUE

Sometimes when I am sad and blue:

_____

Some things that make me sad, and why:

1. _____

_____

_____

_____

_____

_____

_____

_____

_____

2. _____

_____

_____

_____

_____

_____

3. _____

_____

_____

_____

_____

_____

_____

_____

4. _____

_____

_____

_____

_____

_____

_____

_____

_____

_____

Whenever I'm Feeling
SCARED...

Here are some ways I can make myself feel better:

1. Sometimes if I am scared in the dark, I turn on the light. Then I grab my bestest stuffed animal named Philip Johnny Bob. And then both of us sing, "The sun will come out tomorrow" from the hit musical ANNIE.

2. Sometimes I think of a happy memory that makes me laugh . . . like the time me and Grampa Frank Miller had a skipping contest in the grocery store. Only too bad for us, because my grandma spotted us in the frozen food row. And then she took us to the car and made us have a time-out. Only guess what? There were lollipops in

the glove compartment! ha!

3. Other times when I'm scared, I close my eyes very, very tight. And I fill up my 'magination with pictures of GIANT treats! Like sometimes I think of a giant duughnut that's as big as my whole entire house. And then I imagine that it's raining rainbow sprinkles on that tasty thing! Mmm! Mmm! Or other times, I think of a giant ice cream sundae that's so big it fills up my whole bathtub! And then I imagine how fun it would be to put on my bathing suit and dive right into the middle of it. ha! That would be delicious, I think! Plus also, it would be very freezy. And so good news! Time for the hot fudge sauce!

Whenever I'm Feeling
SCARED...

Here are some ways I can make
myself feel better:

THIS IS ME
WHEN I'M SCARED.

1. _____

_____

_____

_____

_____

_____

2. _____

_____

_____

_____

_____

_____

_____

_____

3. _____

_____

_____

_____

_____

_____

_____

_____

_____

_____

_____

_____

_____

_____

_____

_____

Be HAPPY!

Something that always makes me happy is:

When me and Mother and Daddy play Candy Land together and I beat the pants off them.

When I am my happiest, I feel like: I ate a chuckle sandwich.

Happiness makes the corners of my mouth turn up in a big, beautiful:

grin kind of a thing.

Three things I do when I'm happy are:

1. My feet jump way high in the air.
2. I twirl and dance.
3. My arms feel like hugging someone.

The best thing about smiling at people is that they almost always pound you on your **back.**
(I didn't actually get this one.)

The best word to describe how happiness feels is:

WHEEEEEEEEEE!

If you were in a room with friendly aliens
from another planet, how would you
show them you were happy to be there?

Yeah, only here's the problem. I
wouldn't actually be happy to be
there, probably. 'Cause what if the
aliens are just PRETENDING to be
friendly? Huh? Did anyone think of
that? 'Cause aliens aren't all like E.T.,
you know. And so maybe when I'm not
looking, one of them will hit me in the
head with a laser gun or something.
   And so at first, I would just shake
their hands very polite and keep my
head covered. Then, after a while, if
they really, really turned out to be
nice, I would jump and dance. Plus I
might hug them, possibly.

Be HAPPY!

Something that always makes me happy is:

_____

_____

_____

When I am my happiest, I feel like: _____

_____

THIS IS ME
WHEN I'M HAPPY.

Happiness makes the corners of my

mouth turn up in a big, beautiful:

_____

_____

Three things I do when I'm happy are:

1. _____

2. _____

3. _____

The best thing about smiling at people is that they

almost always _____ back.

_____

The best word to describe how happiness feels is:

_____

If you were in a room with friendly aliens
from another planet, how would you
show them you were happy to be there?

_____

_____
_____

_____

_____

_____

_____

_____

_____

_____

_____

_____

_____

_____

_____

_____

A Name Game Starring ME!

Names can tell a lot about you!
Print the letters of your name in the shapes
below. Then fill in a word that
describes yourself starting with each letter!

J — jokey!

U — underwear wearer!

N — not naughty (hardly)!

I — itchy tickle feet!

E — eyeballs need glasses!

B — baby Ollie's BIG sister!

3 Things I Shine At!

1.

The first thing I shine at is when I lick my shoes. 'Cause lick makes them look gleamy.

Shine means good, I think . . . plus also, it means polish.

2.

Another time I shine is when Mother puts the color of clear on my fingernails.

3.

The third thing I shine at is one time I shined my teacher's shoes with my napkin. Only he did not actually like that, I think.

A Name Game Starring ME!

Names can tell a lot about you!
Print the letters of your name in the shapes
below. Then fill in a word that
describes yourself starting with each letter!

3 Things I Shine At!

1.

2.

3.

The PERFECT Birthday!

What if you could have the most PERFECT birthday ever?

1. Would you have a party? If so, where? Of course I would have a party, you sillyhead! I would have it right in my very own backyard. On account of that would be easiest for people to come to. Or else maybe I might have it at the North Pole.

2. Who would you invite? I would invite a million people. 'Cause a million is a nice amount of presents, I think.

Here is a list of the people who I am NOT inviting:

    1. Tattletale May

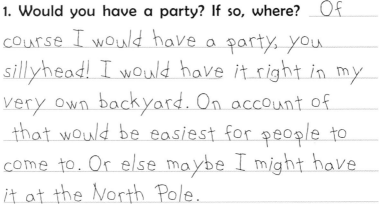

3. If you could invite one famous person to your party, who would it be, and why? I would invite Larry King Live. 'Cause everyone seems to know that guy, except me.

4. What kind of cake would you have? I would have chocolate cake with chocolate icing and chocolate flowers and chocolate candles. The milk will be just plain white. 'Cause too much chocolate is not good for you.

5. What presents would you ask for? I would ask for a canopy bed again. On account of I've asked for that bed for two birthdays in a row already. And so if Mother and Daddy think I am giving up now, they are kidding theirselves.

Also, I am willing to accept cash.

The PERFECT Birthday!

What if you could have the most PERFECT birthday ever?

1. Would you have a party? If so, where? _____

_____

_____

_____

_____

_____

_____

_____

2. Who would you invite? _____

_____

_____

_____

_____

_____

_____

_____

3. If you could invite one famous person to your party, who would it be, and why? _____

_____

_____

_____

4. What kind of cake would you have? _____

_____

_____

_____

_____

5. What presents would you ask for? _____

_____

_____

_____

_____

_____

_____

Two More Freebies!

Still have more you want to write?
Here are two more free pages
to say anything you want!

1. Yay! I am glad to see another freebie page! 'Cause I have another embarrassing thing I want to write about.

   I never actually told anybody this before. But last winter, I had a little bit of a cold. And so one night while I was sleeping, I dreamed that my sheet was a tissue, apparently. 'Cause when I woke up, I was wiping my nose on that thing. And so I quick grabbed a Kleenex. But what do you know? Philip Johnny Bob already saw what I did. And he made a sick face at my sheet. And he said the word EW. Plus then he got out of bed and he slept on the floor.

    I did not actually appreciate that.

2. Here is something very good to tell about myself. I can keep a secret better than anybody I know, almost. Like if you told me your privatest secret in the whole entire world, I would never, ever tell one single person, I bet. Plus also, I would not write it down and send it in the mail, probably.

3. Hey, that reminds me! Here is my privatest secret in the whole world! I think I (love) my bestest friend named (Herbert) He is a nice one, I tell you. Only too bad for me. 'Cause Herb thinks we are just plain friends. And so I will just have to let him keep thinking that until we get married.

Two More Freebies!

Still have more you want to write?
Here are two more free pages
to say anything you want!

_____

_____

_____

_____

_____

_____

_____

_____

_____

_____

_____

_____

_____

_____

_____

_____

_____

_____

Generous Genie Inside!

Did you ever wish you had a magic lamp with a genie inside? (We mean a REALLY generous genie who would grant you 4 wishes instead of the usual 3!)

If you had your own generous genie, what 4 wishes would you choose?

1. First, I would wish that I could turn invisible whenever I wanted to. 'Cause I can think of a jillion times when being invisible would come in handy. Like today at breakfast, I accidentally talked back to Mother. And then I got sent to my room. But if I was invisible, I could stay at the table and make faces at her. And that would be a hoot.

2. Second, I wish I had a teensy little eye in the back of my head. It would be so little that nobody could see it. And so whenever someone made a face

at me, I would yell, "Hey! I saw that!"
And that would scare them silly.

3. Next, I wish that I could fly. Only
I don't want to fly as fast as a jet
plane. I just want to fly slow, like a
bird. 'Cause if I flew as fast as a jet
plane, when I got to where I was
going, I'd be a total wreck.

4. My last wish is that I could
breathe underwater. On account of
then I could swim forever and ever
across the ocean. Plus also, I could
dive way deep down in the water.
And I could find sunken treasure. And
popcorn shrimp.

Generous Genie Inside!

Did you ever wish you had a magic lamp with a genie inside? (We mean a REALLY generous genie who would grant you 4 wishes instead of the usual 3!)

If you had your own generous genie, what 4 wishes would you choose?

1. _____

_____

_____

_____

_____

_____

_____

2. _____

_____

_____

_____

3. _____

4. _____

Time to Say Goodbye!

1. How would you rate your journal experience?

		✓
HO-HUM	**PRETTY GOOD**	**YEE-HAAAA!**

2. Which parts did you like best? I liked the friends' picnic story. Plus also, I liked the part where I was queen of the school.

3. Now that you're done . . . how does it feel to be a real live author? It feels like I'm tired of writing, that's how it feels. And so now I think I will read what I wrote. 'Cause reading is more relaxing to your brain than writing.

Put your official author's signature here:

Junie B. Jones

P.S. Thank you, journal! Plus thank you to my friend who filled out all the other pages. I couldn't have done this book without you!

Time to Say Goodbye!

1. How would you rate your journal experience?

HO-HUM	PRETTY GOOD	YEE-HAAAA!

2. Which parts did you like best? _____

_____

_____

_____

3. Now that you're done . . . how does it feel to

be a real live author? _____

_____

_____

_____

_____

Put your official author's signature here:

_____

Turn to the next page and find fun stickers!

You can use them to decorate your journal!

Hey! Guess what? I stuck a page of stickers
in here for you, too! Most of them are from
the sticker booth at the mall. But some
of them are from my own personal sticker
collection. The toilet is my favorite! ha!
I hope you like them!